D1454987

It's five years since Ben Tennyson last transformed into aliens and fought crime with his cousin Gwen and their Grandpa Max.

Now 15 years old, Ben is once again forced to turn to the Omnitrix to help fight a new and more sinister threat – the HighBreed, DNAliens and the Forever Knights, who team up to take over the world.

The watch-like Omnitrix has re-programmed itself and has a complete set of ten, brand new alien choices for Ben to get to grips with. Helped by his cousin Gwen with her magical powers and Ben's former enemy, Kevin E. Levin, Ben is soon all set to go hero once again!

NOW READ ON . . .

EGMONT

We bring stories to life

This edition first published in Great Britain 2010
by Egmont UK Limited
239 Kensington High Street
London W8 6SA

Adapted by Barry Hutchison

1 3 5 7 9 10 8 6 4 2

Printed and bound in Great Britain

The Forest Stewardship Council (FSC) is an international,
non-governmental organisation dedicated to promoting
responsible management of the world's forests. FSC operates
a system of forest certification and product labelling that
allows consumers to identify wood and wood-based products
from well-managed forests.

For more information about Egmont's paper buying policy,
please visit www.egmont.co.uk/ethicalpublishing
For more information about the FSC, please visit their
website at www.fsc.org

DARKSTAR RISING

CHAPTER ONE

UNDER ARREST

A familiar green and black car crept along a city street, its headlights shining brightly in the darkness. Gravel crunched beneath its wheels as the car pulled off the road and rolled to a stop beside an old warehouse.

The engine fell silent and three figures stepped out of the car. They stood close together, looking up at the blacked-out windows of the warehouse.

'Ben, are you sure this is the right place?' asked Kevin, looking around.

Ben nodded. 'That's what the tip said.'

'Yeah, that's what worries me. You don't get tips. I get tips. You've got no connections.'

'C'mon, Kevin,' Ben protested, 'I've got

tons of connections.'

'Yeah?' sneered Kevin. 'Like who?'

'Um . . .' Ben glanced at his cousin, who was standing just behind Kevin. 'Gwen.'

Gwen nodded, fighting the urge to smile. 'It's true. He does know me.'

'Lot of support there, Gwen,' Ben sighed.

Ignoring her cousin, Gwen began walking towards the warehouse. At the wave of Gwen's hand a series of glowing energy platforms appeared before her, leading up to the roof of the warehouse. She walked up them, with Ben and Kevin following close behind.

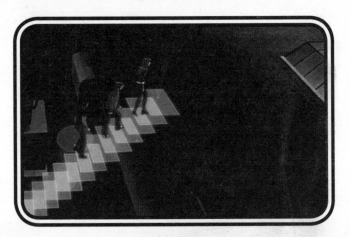

The roof itself was flat, and sturdy enough for them all to walk on. Right in the centre, a raised skylight window allowed them to see what was happening inside. Twenty or more men in silver armour were loading boxes into vans. From where they were standing there was no way of knowing what was in the boxes, but they could guess it was nothing good.

'Forever Knights,' Kevin growled, brushing his hand against the concrete surface of the roof. Almost at once his skin took on the rough grey appearance of the concrete.

'Probably up to no good as usual,' said Gwen, letting sparks of energy crackle across her fingertips.

Beside her, Ben was adjusting the dial on the Omnitrix. He slammed his hand down and an incredible transformation began. Curls of green mist swirled around him as his DNA started to change. His limbs grew longer. His two eyes merged into one. Huge spikes of purple rock grew from his back, until Ben had become the alien known as . . .

'ChromaStone!'

ChromaStone launched himself up into the air. Tucking his knees up to his chest, he dropped like a stone towards the skylight window.

KA-RAAAASH!

The glass exploded, showering the warehouse with deadly shards. A spider-web pattern of cracks appeared on the concrete floor as ChromaStone's feet slammed hard against it.

A second thud shook the warehouse as Kevin dropped down to join ChromaStone. A second later, Gwen floated down on an energy platform and stood shoulder to shoulder with the rest of the team.

'Nobody move!' bellowed ChromaStone.

Around the heroes, the Forever Knights continued to load up the lorries exactly as they had been doing. None of them even turned to look at the towering alien and his two companions.

'Hey,' said Kevin, 'did you guys hear us?'

Gwen frowned, watching a knight casually wheel a trolley of boxes towards them. 'I don't think so,' she said.

Reaching out a hand, Gwen tried to touch the knight on the arm. Instead, her fingers passed straight through him, as if he wasn't there. They all turned and watched as the knight continued on his way.

'Holograms,' gasped ChromaStone.

'Good guess,' boomed a voice.

With a faint fizzle sound, the knights, trucks and boxes all disappeared, leaving the warehouse empty.

Or almost empty.

A tall, powerfully built figure in futuristic armour stepped out from behind a pillar. He slipped the hologram projector into his utility belt. Most of his face was covered, but an area around his mouth could be seen. The skin was green and as rough as sandpaper. Whoever the man was, he wasn't human.

'Who are you?' demanded ChromaStone. 'Don't come any closer!'

'I am Magister Gilhil of the Plumbers,' he said, introducing himself. 'I'm the commanding officer of this entire quadrant.'

Gilhil took a step closer to the group and slowly raised his Plumber badge. 'You're all under arrest,' he told them, 'for impersonating officers of the law.'

In the blink of an eye ChromaStone transformed back into human form. 'Under arrest for what?' Ben demanded.

'Impersonating a Plumber,' Gilhil replied. He was almost double Ben's height and loomed over the boy like a giant. 'We're the only law enforcement organisation recognised by all signatories of the Milky Way treaty. That makes what you've done an interstellar-class felony.'

'Sounds bad,' sneered Kevin, who had barely understood a word the Plumber had said.

Gilhil's mouth pulled into a big scowl. 'Hey, if I were you, kid, I'd keep my mouth in check,' he warned.

Kevin's eyes narrowed. 'If I were you, I wouldn't threaten a guy who could kick your can halfway up the street and back.'

'You feeling froggy, son?' growled Gilhil, clenching his powerful fists. 'Then jump.'

Kevin tensed, but Gwen caught him by the shoulder and held him back. 'If you're feeling smart,' she whispered, 'don't.'

For a moment Kevin hesitated. But only for a moment. Throwing himself at the alien he swung with his solid stone fist. He was going to enjoy pounding on this guy. He was going to –

Kevin barely saw Gilhil move, but the big alien easily caught Kevin's fist in the palm of his hand. With a crack he twisted hard, bending Kevin's wrist backwards. By the time Kevin felt the pain he was already tumbling head-first through the air, straight towards the wall.

KRUNCH!

Kevin thudded against the wall, cracking the plaster. He groaned as he landed heavily on the warehouse floor, but in less than a second he was struggling back to his feet.

Gilhil towered above him. 'Stay down, son,' ordered the alien, but following orders had never been Kevin's style.

Touching the heavy warehouse door, Kevin absorbed its strength. The dull grey of his concrete skin became the shiny silver of metal. If the alien wanted a fight, then Kevin was going to give him one!

Lunging, Kevin swung with his left fist, then his right. Both blows crunched into Gilhil's jaw, stunning him and sending him stumbling backwards. Kevin felt a flash of triumph and prepared to attack again.

'Much as I'd enjoy going a few more rounds with you, I don't have the time,' said Gilhil, pulling a gun from inside his armour.

Before Kevin could react, the alien pulled the trigger. An energy rope launched from the end of the weapon and wrapped itself around Kevin's body, pinning his legs together and binding his hands to his sides. The world seemed to lurch suddenly, as Kevin found himself flipped upside down by the rope and lifted into the air.

Gilhil spun on the spot, pointing his gun at Ben, who was about to activate the Omnitrix. 'Don't,' he warned.

'Do!' cried Gwen, throwing up her hands.

Ben slammed down the Omnitrix's control dial and a cloud of green circled around him. Gilhil's finger twitched on the trigger of his gun, and another energy rope flew at Ben. A crackle of pink energy exploded from Gwen's fingers, blasting the rope to pieces.

Gwen bought her cousin the time he needed. With a gloopy shlopp he transformed into the slimy green alien he called Goop.

Moving like a living puddle, he oozed across the floor and wrapped himself around Gilhil's body, just as the Plumber's rope had done to Kevin.

Gilhil struggled with all his strength, but no matter how hard he wrestled, Goop's grip grew tighter and tighter. With a groan of pain, the Plumber staggered sideways and crashed down onto the floor.

'So you want to talk?' snarled Goop. 'Let's talk!'

CHAPTER TWO

A WARNING

Just a few minutes later, Ben, Gwen and Kevin were standing on the roof. Between them stood Magister Gilhil. He looked angry, but not quite as angry as Kevin.

'I don't see why we gotta talk to him,' Kevin snarled.

'Because I'm the Plumber officer in charge of this whole section of space.'

'Then you know we're the good guys,' said Ben.

Gilhil glared at him. 'What I know is that over the last couple of months, I've gotten several reports of you kids passing yourself off as Plumbers.'

'Our grandfather was a Plumber,' explained Gwen.

'Max Tennyson. He was a good man,' said Gilhil, fondly. His face hardened again. 'But that doesn't make you Plumbers.' He turned to look at Kevin. 'And you don't even have a claim by blood.'

'Yes I do,' snapped Kevin. 'My father, my real father, was . . .' He stopped himself before he could finish the sentence.

Gwen frowned. She'd never heard Kevin talk about his father before. 'Kevin . . .?' she asked, gently.

'Nothing,' muttered Kevin, hanging his head. 'Never mind.'

'The point is, there's a reason we shut down Plumber operations on Earth five years ago,' said Gilhil. 'After Vilgax was destroyed –'

'Surely you mean after I destroyed him,' smiled Ben.

Gilhil nodded. 'Credit due. But Earth is a backwater Level Two planet. Without an imminent threat, I can't allow Plumber resources to be wasted here. I've got over three hundred inhabited planets under my watch.'

'Look, Magister,' began Ben, stepping forward. 'Can I call you Magister?'

'We met another Plumber called Magister once,' said Gwen. 'Magister Labrid.'

Gilhil snorted with laughter. 'Magister is a rank, not a name. You pretend to be Plumbers but you know nothing about the job.'

'I've never pretended to be anything,' replied Gwen, her voice rising.

'Aliens are attacking our planet. We're just fighting to keep it safe,' said Ben.

The Plumber shook his head. 'I've read a number of reports on your activities. There is no evidence of significant alien activity here.'

'We've seen them!' cried Ben.

Gilhil continued, ignoring Ben's protests. 'I've assigned a new Magister to this region. He'll check in on Earth some time in the next few months. If you have proof, present it to him, and let him take care of Plumber business.'

Ben gasped. 'A few months?'

The huge alien looked around the group, deciding what to do next. 'I'm inclined to give you kids a break,' he said at last. 'Ben, you wear the Omnitrix so you already have special dispensation. The Galvin have requested that you are not interfered with in minor matters.'

Ben was surprised by this. The Galvin were a race of small, super-intelligent aliens. One of them – a scientist named Azmuth – had created the Omnitrix, but Ben always got the feeling that Azmuth didn't like him very much. He was the last person Ben expected to be looking out for him.

Even as Ben thought about this, Gilhil had turned to face Gwen. 'The reports I've read indicate that, as you say, you've never impersonated a Plumber,' he told her. 'But you . . .' he began, rounding on Kevin.

'Yeah, what?'

'You've got a record. You've done time in the Null Void for a variety of crimes.'

'He's changed,' insisted Gwen.

'He's been helping us,' agreed Ben.

'He's been impersonating a Plumber,' Gilhil snapped. He held out a hand that looked strong enough to crush solid rock. 'Give me the badge you stole.'

Kevin's eyes went wide. 'No way. Come on, don't take my badge, man,' he begged, looking to Ben and Gwen for support. 'Please.'

'Now!' demanded Gilhil, 'or you're going back to the Null Void.'

For a moment Kevin hesitated, considering his options. Then, slowly, he reached into his pocket, took out his Plumber badge, and passed it to Gilhil.

'Thank you. You're free to go,' Gilhil announced. 'But if you ever get involved in Plumber business again, you're all going to the Null Void. Even you, Ben.'

The Plumber flicked a switch on his armour and was suddenly surrounded by hundreds of twinkling lights. The lights grew brighter and brighter until, in a sudden flash, Gilhil teleported away.

For several long moments Ben, Gwen and Kevin stood in silence. The only sound was the soft whistling of the breeze and the faint rumbling of distant traffic.

It was Ben who finally said what they were all thinking. 'Is that it?' he asked. 'Is this the end?'

Ben pushed open the door and stepped out of the Mr Smoothy store, sipping from a huge paper cup. Two other cups were balanced on a cardboard tray. Ben slurped down his drink as he strolled across the car park. Eventually he reached Kevin's car. Kevin and Gwen were sat on the bonnet, looking miserable.

'Cheer up,' smiled Ben, before letting out an enormous burp. 'Mr Smoothy makes everything better.'

He handed a cup to Kevin, and one to Gwen. Kevin took a sip, then pulled a disgusted face. 'How does turnip and wheatgrass sludge make anything better?'

SCHLUUURP!

Ben drained the rest of his cup in one go. 'Well, I like it,' he said. 'Besides, it's also got ginger in it.'

Gwen stopped with the straw half-way to her lips. She thought about the ingredients, imagined how they would taste, and then quietly sat her cup down on the ground.

'Oh, ginger,' scowled Kevin. 'Now that solves all our problems.'

'Seriously, Ben,' added Gwen. 'Magister Gilhil pretty much just put us out of business. What are we gonna do?'

Ben hopped up so he was sitting beside his cousin. 'We're gonna keep doing what we've been doing. Find the aliens, fight the bad guys.'

'He said he'd put us in the Null Void,' Gwen reminded him.

'Yeah, but he also said that Plumbers never come around here any more. So we'll worry about it when, or should I say if, he ever shows up again.'

Kevin gave a sigh. 'He took my badge.'

'Badges?' laughed Ben. 'We don't need no stinkin' badges!'

Springing to his feet, Kevin slammed his hand against Ben's chest and caught him by his jacket. 'You think this is a joke?' he growled.

'Kevin, let him go,' cried Gwen.

With a grunt, Kevin released his grip and turned away. 'I wanna be a Plumber, OK?' he mumbled. 'When I was little, my mum would tell me stories about my dad. How he was a Plumber and did all this cool stuff.'

Gwen rested a hand on his shoulder. 'I never met your dad.'

'Me neither,' said Kevin. 'But I still wanna be like him.'

'That's why you know so much about the Plumbers and alien technology and everything,' Gwen realised.

'It's why I agreed to help you guys in the first place.' He turned and looked deep into Gwen's eyes. 'Mostly.'

Gwen opened her mouth to reply, but Kevin had already pulled away. He yanked open the door to his car and climbed inside.

'I've got to get my badge back,' he told them, turning the ignition key and revving the engine. 'It's the only thing that matters.'

Ben barely had time to jump down from the bonnet before Kevin slammed his door shut and hit the accelerator. The car lurched forward and sped off into the distance, leaving Ben and Gwen far behind.

CHAPTER THREE

DARKSTAR ATTACKS

Many miles away from Mr Smoothy, strange alien figures scuttled around a darkened cave, carrying equipment to and from the enormous spaceship that lurked beside them in the dark cavern. They were DNAliens, the servants of the HighBreed.

And they were not alone.

A figure emerged from the shadows, dressed all in black. A metal mask covered his face and head. The mask was blank, aside from two slits for eyes and a larger one for a mouth. As he walked through the cave, a few DNAliens moved to block his path.

The strange figure grabbed the DNAliens and threw them to the ground.

CRASH!

Four of the aliens began to hack and cough. Then, with a horrible retching sound, they spat up football-sized lumps of sticky green goo. The goo-balls shot across the cave, directly towards the masked stranger.

BZZZZZAP!

Powerful blasts of dark energy exploded from the stranger's fingertips. As the blasts hit the goo-balls, they burned up and vanished into dust. The DNAliens began to cough up more gunk, but they were too late. Another blast of dark energy struck the ground by their feet, sending them sprawling backwards onto the cave floor.

Behind his mask, the mysterious stranger smiled. His name was Darkstar, and hurting people was what he did best.

Striding past the unconscious aliens, Darkstar approached the entrance to the spaceship. The thick metal door was closed, but that didn't matter to him. Darkstar had come here for one reason, and nothing was going to get in his way.

Punching his gloved hands against the door frame, Darkstar dug his fingers into the hole his blows created. With a grunt of effort he pulled hard on the door. The metal creaked, then tore free with an ear-splitting crash.

Laser blasts streaked along the spaceship corridor, catching Darkstar by surprise. They hit him in the chest, throwing him backwards and forcing him to throw his hands up in front of his face.

Along the corridor, a squadron of DNAliens advanced, squeezing the triggers of their laser guns, blasting the intruder again and again. They communicated anxiously in their alien language, shouting to make themselves heard above the screaming of their weapons.

Darkstar didn't know what the aliens were saying and he didn't care. They had taken him by surprise, but he had recovered quickly. They were no longer a threat to him. They were simply annoying.

With a flick of his wrist he sent bolts of energy screeching towards the oncoming aliens. The blasts moved too quickly for the DNAliens to dodge them. Several voices cried out in pain. Several guns clattered to the ground. And then there was no sound in the corridor, but the soft thudding of Darkstar's footsteps.

Half-way along the corridor, Darkstar heard another sound. It was soft and faint and coming from directly above him. Reaching up with one hand, he caught the DNAlien who had been preparing to leap down on top of him. Without even slowing down, he slammed the creature head-first against the ground, and turned the corner at the corridor's end.

More DNAliens lay in wait, their weapons raised and ready to fire. Darkstar sighed. This was becoming boring. Very boring. Raising his hands he unleashed a rain of dark energy. In less than a second, not a single alien was left standing.

Stepping over their bodies, Darkstar approached the door they had been guarding. Behind his mask his eyes blazed with excitement. This was it. This was the moment he had been waiting for.

The metal door collapsed with a single shove, and the masked figure stepped through the hole that was left in its place. Across the room a high-backed chair spun around, revealing a HighBreed alien.

'Who are you?' demanded the alien, leaping to his feet. 'And what insignificant alien speck dares to enter the command centre of a HighBreed Lord?'

He was easily twice as tall as Darkstar, and from the way he spoke it was obvious that he was very angry.

Darkstar didn't reply. Instead he kept walking, each step bringing him closer and closer to the hulking alien.

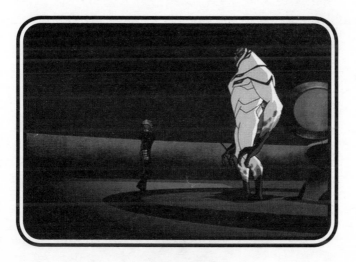

'It doesn't matter,' snorted the HighBreed. 'Dead men don't need names.'

THWACK!

A crunching back-hand caught Darkstar on the side of the head and sent him crashing into a bank of computer monitors. The equipment exploded beneath him, bringing a mound of rock and broken metal down on top of his head.

Darkstar got to his feet, brushing the heavy equipment away as if it were made of cardboard. 'Nice shot,' he said, picking up a heavy boulder and raising it above his head. 'You're just as strong as I'd heard.'

The HighBreed braced himself for battle, but his opponent was already on the attack. Darkstar hurled the boulder with all his strength. It flipped twice in the air, then found its target. The HighBreed roared in pain and rage as he was knocked to the ground.

But the alien wasn't beaten yet. Pushing

the rock aside he began to climb to his feet, his diamond-shaped eyes fixed on his enemy. The HighBreed tensed his huge muscles, preparing to fight.

Beneath his mask, Darkstar licked his lips. 'That's it,' he hissed, raising his hand. 'Show me all of your power!'

A band of black energy snaked from Darkstar's fingertips. It wrapped around the HighBreed and seemed to burrow through the alien's skin.

'Give me your strength.'

The HighBreed howled and thrashed around as Darkstar drained the power from his body. He tried to fight, but he was weakening too quickly. With a final cry of pain, the huge alien collapsed, face first, to the ground.

After taking a moment to enjoy the taste of the HighBreed's powerful energy, Darkstar crossed to the fallen alien and poked him with the toe of his boot. The HighBreed rolled over onto his back and groaned.

'What do you want from me?'

Darkstar crouched down so his mask was just a few centimetres away from the alien's face. 'I want,' he said, 'to make a deal.'

Kevin twisted the spanner, tightening a part of his car's engine that had been tight enough to begin with. There was nothing wrong with the car, but he liked tinkering with it. It helped him to think.

He was so busy thinking he almost didn't hear the footsteps approaching his garage until it was too late.

'Who's out there?' he growled, peering out into the darkness beyond the garage door.

For a moment nothing happened, and then Gwen appeared, a plastic cup in each hand. 'Me,' she said with a smile. 'I brought you something to drink.'

Kevin shuddered. 'Yeah, but no thanks. I'm fine.'

'It's not a smoothie,' Gwen said, taking a sip from one of the cups. 'See? Regular soda.'

She held the cup out to Kevin. He hesitated for a moment, before taking it from her. 'OK,' he said, before taking a long drink.

'I just wanted to see how you were doing,' said Gwen.

'Fine,' Kevin took a deep breath. 'Listen, I don't want to talk about my dad.'

'Never crossed my mind,' Gwen replied. 'I brought you a present.' She pulled a small bag from her pocket. Reaching inside she pulled out a small ball and tossed it to Kevin.

'What's this?' he asked, catching the ball and studying it.

'A wooden ball. Absorb it.'

Kevin shrugged and absorbed the

properties of the ball. At once his hand became a dark shade of brown.

'How about this one?' asked Gwen, throwing him another. 'It's a ball bearing. Made out of, I dunno, ball bearing stuff.'

'Stainless steel.'

'I brought you a whole bag of them, all made of different materials,' Gwen told him. 'That way, when we're in a fight, you can change to whatever you want.'

'Thanks, but it doesn't really work that way,' replied Kevin, taking the bag. 'I need a lot of whatever I'm copying.'

Gwen looked disappointed. 'Oh.'

'And what makes you think I'm still helping you guys, anyway?'

Taking Kevin's hand, Gwen said, 'Because you've changed.'

'Maybe, but I'm still on parole. That Magister can put me back in the Null Void any time he wants.'

Gwen held Kevin's hand tighter. There was so much she wanted to say to him. If only she could show him how important he was to the team – and to her.

KARAAASH!

A sudden shattering of stone derailed Gwen's train of thought. She and Kevin spun around to face the wall. A large area of brickwork had been torn away. In its place stood the hulking frame of the HighBreed Lord.

'Human scum,' the alien squealed, 'I will cleanse the world of your filth!'

Placing his hands against the floor, Kevin quickly absorbed the properties of the concrete. As his body became as hard as stone, he turned to Gwen. 'Looks like I picked the wrong day to give up fighting monsters.'

CHAPTER FOUR

FRAMED

I t's a HighBreed!' cried Gwen. 'Ben says they're too strong for us to fight.'

'Well, Ben ain't here!'

Kevin darted forwards, his fists clenched. The alien was much taller than he was, and he had to leap upwards to drive two solid punches against the HighBreed's jaw. But the alien barely seemed to notice them.

THWACK!

Lashing out, the HighBreed hit Kevin with a powerful uppercut, sending him backflipping across the garage. With a crash of metal, Kevin smashed into the bonnet of his car, crumpling it. Groaning, Kevin tried to get up, but his arms shook, then folded beneath him.

Stepping in front of her fallen friend, Gwen hit the HighBreed with an energy beam. The pink light wrapped itself around the alien, tightening like a rope around its body.

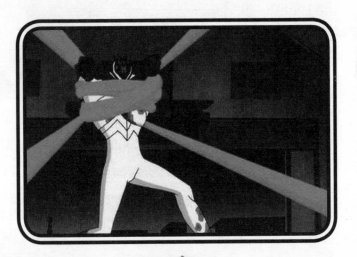

With a shrug of powerful shoulders, the HighBreed shook off the energy beam, sending it rocketing back towards Gwen. Ducking too late, Gwen caught the blast on the side of her head. The world seemed to spin for a moment, before Gwen sunk to the floor, her eyes closed.

Fighting to stay awake, Gwen forced her eyes open again, just in time to see the HighBreed slamming his fists down towards her. Gasping, she threw up an energy shield, just in time to stop the alien crushing her.

'That won't save you, human!' roared the HighBreed, raining blow after deadly blow down on the shield.

Gwen's eyes went wide with horror as the shield began to crack beneath the strain. Finally, with one last punch, the shield flickered and disappeared. The HighBreed cackled loudly as he brought his huge fist down one last time. Gwen screwed her eyes tight shut, bracing herself for the end.

KRUUUNCH!

Gwen opened her eyes again and found herself looking into Kevin's. He kneeled over her, shielding her from the HighBreed's punch. For a moment he tried to smile, and then his eyes rolled back in his head and his rock covering began to crack and crumble.

With a final whimper of pain, Kevin rolled sideways and lay still on the garage floor. Gwen looked up, defenceless now as the HighBreed raised his fists to deliver the final killer blow.

And then, without warning, a hand – even bigger than the alien's – caught the HighBreed by the wrist.

'Hey, ugly,' growled Humungousaur. 'Why don't you pick on somebody your own size?'

Humungousaur spun quickly on the spot, keeping a tight grip on the HighBreed's wrist. Faster and faster the alien hero turned, until he was spinning at just the perfect speed.

With a grunt, Humungousaur launched

the HighBreed up towards the garage ceiling. The roof exploded, showering glass, stone and dust up into the night sky.

Screaming, the HighBreed tumbled through the air, before finally crashing back down to earth with the force of a small meteorite, creating a deep crater in the ground.

At the bottom of the crater, the HighBreed wiped dust from his eyes. His whole body hurt, but that would not stop him. He began to get to his feet. Nothing would stop him. Nothing!

An angry, dinosaur-like face glared down at him from the top of the pit. 'I wouldn't, if I were you,' growled Humungousaur.

The HighBreed swallowed hard. OK, so maybe that would stop him.

Gwen and Kevin – who were both now back on their feet – rushed over to join Humungousaur at the edge of the crater. If the HighBreed decided to keep fighting, then they wanted a piece of the action too.

A voice from nearby took them by surprise. 'Didn't take you kids long to get yourselves into trouble again, did it?'

Humungousaur and the others turned to find Magister Gilhil watching them.

'We were just – ' Humungousaur began.

'Attacking me for no reason,' finished the HighBreed, clambering free of the crater.

'He's one of the aliens we told you about,' argued Kevin. 'He's attacking Earth.'

'How about some proof?' sighed Gilhil.

'They attacked me for no reason,' insisted the HighBreed. 'They said they were Plumbers.'

Gilhil's eyes darkened. 'I've heard enough. You three are under arrest. And you,' he said, turning to the HighBreed, 'I don't know what's going on here, but I'm gonna find out. You're coming with me for questioning.'

'I beg to differ,' boomed another voice. This time it was Darkstar's turn to make a surprise appearance. 'Nobody's going anywhere,' he told them. 'Not until I make your powers my own!'

The night air seemed to sizzle as the dark energy snaked from Darkstar's fingertips. Five bolts shot out, four of them hitting their targets. Only Gwen was fast enough to surround herself with an energy bubble. All around her, the others fell to the ground, writhing in pain as Darkstar drained them of their strength.

'Why me?' cried the HighBreed. 'You promised that if I helped you . . .'

Behind his mask, Darkstar's mouth pulled into a sneer. 'I can't be trusted,' he laughed.

Humungousaur gritted his teeth. He'd never felt such pain before. On his left, Kevin was already knocked out. On his right, Gilhil was also falling unconscious. Gwen was pinned inside her energy bubble. That left only him.

Summoning all his strength, the huge dino-alien took a step towards Darkstar. The pain became worse, but he couldn't give up. He wouldn't. Another step brought him closer to the masked figure. Then another, and another.

'I'd almost forgotten how strong you are,' said Darkstar, shouting to make himself heard over the buzzing of his energy beams. 'Ben.'

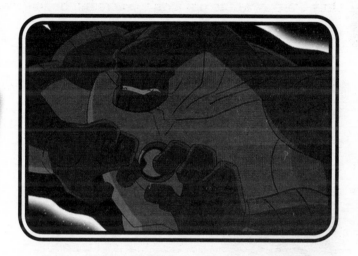

Spreading his fingers wider, he increased the power of his beams. Humungousaur roared in pain. Then in a blur of green, the alien transformed back into Ben.

'Who are you?' Ben gasped, his power still being sapped by Darkstar. 'How did you – ?'

And then, in a blinding flash, the truth hit him. Ben knew now who he was dealing with, and it made his blood run cold.

'Gwen, run!' he cried.

'What?'

'You've got to get away, you're our only hope. Run!'

Gwen hesitated. She didn't like the idea of running out on the others, but there was no way she could stop Darkstar on her own.

With a final glance down at Kevin, Gwen bunched her energy shield up into a ball and sent it rocketing towards Darkstar. It exploded in a blinding light around him.

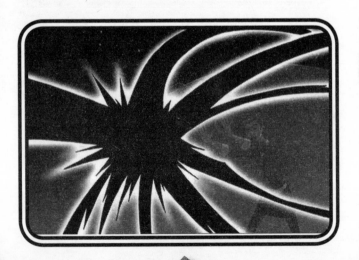

By the time Darkstar's vision had cleared, Gwen was nowhere to be seen.

'You can't run forever, lovely Gwen,' he shouted. 'I'll have my revenge on you, too!'

Darkstar turned and looked down at the four other figures, who were all lying on the ground. A glint lit up his eyes as his gaze fell on Ben and Kevin. 'But first things first . . .'

CHAPTER FIVE

UNEXPECTED ALLIES

Ben forced open his eyes and immediately wished that he hadn't. He was tied with heavy chains and pinned inside a glowing blue energy prison, unable to move. Judging by the equipment around the room, the prison seemed to be inside a power plant, but he couldn't say for sure. Beside him, Kevin, Gilhil and the HighBreed were trapped in the same way.

'I don't understand what's going on,' groaned Gilhil. 'That's the guy who tipped me off that you were impersonating Plumbers.'

Kevin grunted. 'And he scammed big ugly, too.'

The HighBreed growled at him.

'I know who he is,' Ben announced.

'Do you really?' boomed Darkstar, who had been standing nearby, watching on.

'You have to be somebody who knows all about the Plumbers and the HighBreed,' Ben replied. 'But most importantly, you have to be someone with a grudge against us. Why don't you take off the dopey mask, Mike?'

'That's Mike Morningstar?' splutted Kevin. 'The creep who tried to steal Gwen from . . .' He stopped just in time to avoid saying anything embarrassing. 'Who stole his powers from all those girls at his school?'

'When you ruined my plan, you nearly destroyed me,' Darkstar said. 'But my powers returned, stronger than ever. As did my hunger. My old method of feeding is not enough.'

'High school girls too tough for you, huh?' snorted Ben.

'To the contrary, my friends. I need more power than they can supply. Mike Morningstar no longer exists.'

With a clatter his metal mask fell to the floor. Ben and Kevin stared in disbelief at the horror standing before them. Mike's once handsome features were now shrivelled and decayed, his skin wrinkled and grey.

'Now I am Darkstar!' he said, enjoying his enemies' horrified reaction. 'You did this to me. And you will feed my hunger.'

More of Darkstar's energy beams shot from his hands. They passed easily through the force field and wrapped around the four prisoners. The captives cried out in pain.

'I will take your strength and make it my own, until you have no more to give.'

Kevin fought against the pain. 'Ben, if you can reach your Omnitrix,' he mumbled, 'maybe Alien X – '

Ben shook his head. 'No. If he absorbed all that power, nothing could stop him.'

'Eventually, I'll have it all anyway,' said Darkstar, grinning.

From close behind him, Darkstar heard a faint cough. He turned around, only to find Gwen standing inside the doorway. She was leaning against the wall, her arms folded.

'Ew,' winced Gwen, when she saw Darkstar's face. 'I swear you were better looking when we used to go out.'

'Laugh while you can,' Darkstar hissed. 'I've got all the power of your teammates, plus the HighBreed and the Plumber. How can you possibly hope to defeat me alone?'

Gwen raised an eyebrow. 'Who said anything about "alone"?'

As if on cue, the windows of the room exploded inwards, as dozens of DNAliens came crashing through. Yet more of them swarmed in through the door behind Gwen.

'They're pretty mad at you for kidnapping their boss,' said Gwen, just as the first wave of DNAliens launched an attack on Darkstar. Darkstar reacted quickly, knocking them back with an energy blast. But another group were already launching a second assault, forcing Darkstar to fire wildly as he struggled to keep them all back.

From across the room Gwen fired an energy beam of her own. It hit the force field projector, frying the electrics inside. The prison walls flickered for a moment, then disappeared.

Absorbing the metal of the chains around him, Kevin turned his body into living iron. Flexing his metallic muscles he snapped the chain, and set about freeing Ben and Gilhil.

'Thanks, kid,' said the Plumber as his chains were torn away.

'What about me?' said the HighBreed.

'Hang in there,' said Ben with a smirk.

Just a few metres away, Darkstar was grappling with a DNAlien. Placing his hand against its head he drained its energy away. The power tasted good, but the aliens had surrounded him and were moving in to attack.

'Too many to absorb,' he muttered.

'And the bad news keeps on coming,' said Gwen, raising her hands.

A circle of pink energy thundered into Darkstar, sending him tumbling into the wall. He was spinning too fast to notice the flash of green energy as Ben transformed into the alien known as Echo Echo.

Opening his mouth wide, Echo Echo hit
Darkstar with a sonic blast, catapulting him
high up into the air. Gilhil drew his weapon
and took aim. With a squeeze of the trigger he
blasted Darkstar with a laser bolt, taking some
of the fight out of him.

But Darkstar wasn't done yet. He raised
his arms, preparing to unleash his dark energy.
From the corner of his eye he spotted a burst
of green light, and turned just in time to see
Spidermonkey swinging towards him.

Spidermonkey's feet slammed hard

against Darkstar's jaw, sending him plummeting towards the ground. Even as Spidermonkey fell after him, the Omnitrix energy swirled around, changing him into yet another alien form.

Jet Ray raised his tail and fired a stream of green energy at Darkstar, blasting him just as he crunched against the concrete floor.

Weakened, but determined to win the fight, Darkstar tried to get to his feet. Before he could get very far, an enormous shadow loomed over him. Collapsing onto his back, he looked up at the snarling face of Humungousaur.

'Nighty-night,' growled the dino-alien, raising a massive foot.

BADOOOM!

Humungousaur brought his foot down on the fallen figure of Darkstar – not hard enough to kill him, but hard enough to make sure he wouldn't be getting back up any time soon.

With Darkstar finally defeated, Gwen glanced over to where they had left the HighBreed Lord. Only his chains remained.

'The HighBreed is gone,' she sighed.

'The DNAliens must have sprung him while we were fighting,' said Kevin, turning back into his human form. He looked across to Humungousaur, just in time to see him transform back to Ben. 'You OK, man?'

Ben shook his head. 'Tired,' he gasped, before falling to his knees. Gwen caught him.

'Sit down and catch your breath,' she said, guiding him gently to the ground.

Gilhil leaned closer. 'Is he OK?'

'Everything . . . spinning. Double vision. Going dim,' Ben groaned. 'Need . . . smoothie.'

Gwen smiled, relieved. 'He's fine.'

Less than an hour later, all four of the heroes stood outside the power station. Darkstar stood between them, trapped inside an energy prison, his hands bound by laser cuffs.

'Will that rig hold him?' asked Kevin.

'It's Level Six technology,' Gilhil replied. 'He isn't going anywhere but the Null Void.'

'What about us?' asked Ben.

'I've been giving that some thought. You guys made a difference today. Maybe I don't need to reassign good men to this quadrant,' said Gilhil. 'Maybe they're already here.'

Kevin frowned. 'What's that mean?'

'You've been drafted. Here's your badge back.' Gilhil held out a Plumber badge. Kevin took it eagerly. 'And here's one for you,' said Gilhil, passing a badge to Gwen. Ben held out his hand. 'Don't push it, kid. You've already got the Omnitrix.'

Ben couldn't argue with that.

'As of now you're the only law in the quadrant,' Gilhil told them. Lights twinkled around him and Darkstar as they began to teleport away. 'Do a good job.'

And with that, the Plumber vanished.

Ben turned to look at his friends, but Kevin was already walking away.

'Hey, where are you going?'

Kevin glanced back at the others, then looked down at the badge. His badge. He smiled. 'I gotta tell my mum.'